The House That Sailed Away

The House That Sailed Away

Jacqueline Harris

Illustrated by
Alan Brown

Collins

Chapter 1

When Jake Salmon turned ten years old, he got a letter from his father. This might not have been so unusual except that his father had been dead for more than seven years. He'd been lost at sea and Jake could scarcely remember what he looked like.

Jake's grandparents handed him the letter on Jake's tenth birthday, along with the usual cards. They told him what it was and said they'd been looking after it for all these years. The letter was brief, in a scrawled hand, but nice to have anyway.

Dear Jake,

If you're reading this, then I'm not around. The trouble with being at sea is that you never know what might happen, but I wanted you to know I've always been thinking of you and sending you my love, no matter how far away I am.

Ten seems very old to me right now, but I thought it was the right time for you to get a letter. Look after your Mum and "Toledo" and never forget how much I love you.

Dad

PS Don't forget how important the name of the house is to us!

Jake half threw the letter across the table.

"Well, I'm not doing a very good job, am I!" he said. "I'm not looking after Mum, and I don't even know what Toledo is!"

"Your dad couldn't have guessed about your Mum," Grandma told Jake gently. "Toledo was your house, where you used to live when you were little. It's also the place in Spain where your parents had their honeymoon. Your dad loved that house so much – "

"So Dad asked me to do two things and I'm not doing either of them."

Jake saw his grandparents exchange pained looks but felt he had every right to be upset.

Normally, he hardly thought about his mother, but today, even though she'd sent him a card and a book token, he felt angry with her, with his dad and mostly with himself.

"Jake, your dad was just saying what was relevant at the time he wrote the letter. He wouldn't be cross with you or hold you responsible for anything that's happened." It was his grandfather this time, in his quiet, understated way. "He wasn't to know your mum would behave as she did."

Jake saw the old guilty expression creep across Grandpa's face. He always had that expression when he talked about Jake's mother, like it was his fault she'd run off with Tim from next door. Instantly, Jake felt guilty himself; he knew his grandparents tried incredibly hard to make up for both parents not being there, and it was only very occasionally he felt the loss himself. Jake knew he was loved and knew his grandparents cared for him. But then there was that letter, making him feel that he hadn't done what his father wanted, and his birthday seemed somehow less for it.

"So, Toledo's a house," he said. "Where is it?"

"Not far, nearly at the crossroads with Ambridge Road and Crow Road."

Almost as soon as his grandmother said the location, Jake decided he would have to go and see for himself.

"What road and number?" he asked.

"Ambridge Road, number 63. We can go there one day if you like," Grandma offered.

"Nah," Jake muttered, quickly finishing his toast, and getting up to go and grab his things for school. "No point, it's in the past and I didn't look after it, anyway." He paused, making the decision about whether to lie. "I've got running after school, extra practice; I'll be a bit late."

"Do you want a lift home?" Grandpa asked.

Jake shook his head, and mumbled thanks for the offer. Slinging his rucksack over one arm, he went out of the front door, pausing only to call out a goodbye to his grandparents. Then he was off, walking briskly down the road to the corner where Shi would be waiting for him.

Shi was Jake's best friend from his class at school and it would be hard to find a pair who were more different. Shi was tall, with straight dark hair that fell into his eyes; he was also well-known as the boy most likely to get into trouble at school. He was reckless and rushed into things without thinking them through. He was also cheeky and funny, and often the class clown.

Jake was one of the shortest children in the year and had messy, curly hair that never looked brushed; he was also almost never in trouble. Jake often thought Shi was badly named, as he was the least shy person he knew. Shi's family came from Israel, and he was loud and confident, and the youngest of four brothers. Jake loved going to Shi's house; it was everything his own home wasn't, with everyone talking loudly, often in two languages and all at the same time. Jake's grandparents' home was very quiet in comparison.

Shi greeted him enthusiastically, wishing him a

happy birthday, and shoved a card into his hand. "Don't lose it; it has a book token in there. My mum said you'd like that." He spoke as though he thought it was an odd choice of gift.

Jake nodded and tried to smile, but the events of the morning were still going round and round in his head.

"I got a letter from my dad," Jake blurted. "My grandparents have been saving it for me. It didn't say much. I wanted it to say so much more, but I don't know what. Instead, it just made me feel bad." Jake told Shi everything.

They began walking along the road towards school. They crossed the road at the zebra crossing and headed past The Green to Greenside Primary School, which was set back behind the trees. The low buildings almost looked as if they were hiding away, trying not to be seen.

Jake suddenly stopped and bent down to pick up a coin lying on the pavement. *Find a penny, pick it up, all day long, you'll have good luck.* His grandfather said that all the time. He felt he could do with a bit of good luck today.

"What did you get for your birthday?" Shi asked.

"I only opened cards this morning – we do presents in the evening when we're not in a rush." Jake would usually chat the whole way to school, but he didn't feel like talking today.

They went and stood in the playground, waiting for the bell to ring. Mr Poppard came striding out; he was, as always, a few minutes late. Jake liked Mr Poppard, but he felt like he couldn't deal with the jokes or the loudness today. Mr Poppard was very tall and thin, and all the children liked him enormously. He was always enthusiastic and lessons were never dull with him.

"I believe someone has a birthday today," Mr Poppard chuckled, as he walked the class inside. "We'll have to sing to you, Jake!" Mr Poppard clearly had no idea how embarrassing it was to have "Happy Birthday" sung to you at this age.

Jake found everyone looking at him while they sang quite excruciating. He knew most of his classmates pitied him, knowing he had a dead father, and his mother wasn't around. He'd even heard parents talking about him in the playground and caught phrases like "that poor boy" being used. Jake didn't feel like a poor boy, in fact, he knew his home life was nicer than many of his classmates. That morning, however, he really minded the looks and the pity. He minded that Callum Grant was singing a rude version of "Happy Birthday", and that Harrison Smith was giggling instead of singing. He wished Mr Poppard hadn't remembered what day it was and most of all he wished he hadn't received the letter.

At the end of the school day, Jake walked back to the corner with Shi. Once Shi had left him, Jake sprinted past his grandparents' house and on down the road. He walked for about 15 minutes before he saw the road sign, Crow Road. It was time to find the house!

Chapter 2

The houses were mainly big and old, and many had been turned into flats. Jake paused at the crossroads with Ambridge Road and stared. On one side of Ambridge Road, the houses had all been demolished and there was a building site with big signs advertising a new development of three-to-four-bedroom luxury homes. On the other side, the houses were still standing, but they were hidden from view behind lilac hoardings.

Jake hoped the house he once lived in was still standing; that would be worse than awful if he was too late. Jake crossed the road and started to walk along Ambridge Road, peering through the cracks in the boards to see if he could spot number 63. He realised he was going in the wrong direction but, as the numbers were odd on this side of the road, his house would still be there, and he turned back. The road was deserted, and the only sounds were from the building site opposite. He found 61 and then the house he guessed must be 63, set slightly further back than the other houses. The boards weren't entirely closed together and there was a gap just large enough for him to slip through.

Number 63 wasn't a huge house, nor did it look older than any of the other houses. Jake felt it was familiar, even though he didn't really remember living there. The smaller upstairs window had odd brickwork beneath it that made the window look wonky, even though it wasn't. In fact, it made the whole house look a bit crooked.

There was a small front garden, which was overgrown and a large decorative front door with thin panels of stained glass. Jake went up to the door and pushed at it, but it was clearly locked. He looked up at the nameplate next to the door,

on a carved slice of wood, with the name "Toledo" in curling letters.

Something seemed to ring a bell in his head, like the ghost of the past sliding into his thoughts. He thought back to the letter from this morning, that the name of the house was important. He reached up to the sign and felt behind it. He had to stand on tiptoes, but he could just feel the back of the nameplate and there, incredibly, was the front door key. Jake held it in his hand, and wondered why his mother had left it. He went to the front door and slipped it into the lock; it was only a little stiff.

Inside, the house was musty, and the air smelt of dust. Jake remembered the chequerboard tiles in the hallway and the narrow passage towards the kitchen. He closed the front door behind him and went to explore. He walked from room to room, but he couldn't really remember living there. The house seemed heavy with emptiness. Upstairs, he paused when he found what must have been his room; there were bright train stencils and yellow paint on the walls. He walked slowly, hearing his feet on the bare boards, trying hard to recreate in his head what it had been like before.

Then he found another set of stairs going up into an attic room that looked over the garden. The room at the top was bright and had large windows and, oddly, a wooden column in the centre with a ship's wheel and a sort of dashboard and joystick. Under the dashboard was a small cupboard.

Jake was certain he'd never seen this before and he wondered if it had been where his father had kept his Navy things, if he'd had any of those. Jake opened the cupboard to find a little leatherbound notebook, filled with his father's spidery handwriting that he recognised from the letter this morning. It seemed as if it was notes on how to sail a ship.

The dashboard and wheel were covered in layers of dust and Jake used his school sweatshirt to clean it off. He tried to turn the wheel, but it appeared to be locked in place; he studied the dashboard and flicked a switch. There was no noise, only a subtle sense that the house was vibrating ever so slightly, and Jake pulled his hands away from the switch as if it had been hot. As he did so, his arm caught the wheel and this time it moved. The house lurched, and Jake nearly fell over.

As he steadied himself, Jake's first thought was that the house was collapsing and then that the demolition had just started. But the walls showed no cracks and there was silence, apart from a soft hum, almost below his feet. He studied the dashboard carefully. The switch was labelled "ON/OFF", and there was a small, printed nameplate beneath it. The other dials and switches also had small nameplates, but these were letters, like "AN", and he didn't know what they meant. Jake grasped the wheel in both hands and slowly turned it. The house lurched again, but more gently this time. He felt resistance in the movement, as if the house was trying to move but was still attached to the ground. Jake switched the on/off switch to off and the hum stopped.

So, this is why Dad wanted me to take care of the house! he thought. He felt as if he should have been more surprised, after all, this kind of thing didn't happen every day, or at all. Instead, Jake went downstairs and let himself out of the back door, which had the key still in the lock, to go and investigate the base of the house. Maybe the coin had brought an extraordinary, birthday kind of luck.

The back garden was covered in roses and thorns. It was probably quite large, but Jake couldn't see very far through the trees and overgrown tangle. He walked through long grass, looking at the base of the house. He could see the marks where the house had moved slightly; the earth and grass had been churned and flattened. There didn't, however, appear to be any gap under the house, not even a tiny one he could slide his fingers into.

At one corner of the house, there was a huge chain, dangling from below the first-floor window. Jake followed the chain across the grass to where it lay partially submerged in some bushes. He pushed at a large shrub and found the end of the chain which had a huge anchor attached to it. *Well, that explains it,* he thought.

Running back into the house, careful to lock the back door behind him, Jake took the stairs two at a time. Reaching the attic room out of breath, he paused at the window to look over the back garden. If he pressed his nose against the glass, he could just make out where the anchor lay.

Jake picked up the notebook and leafed through it. What if the instructions weren't for a boat, they were for the house! Each of the switches were in the book and there were notes by some of them. Even without the notebook, Jake could now guess that "AN" meant anchor. Jake flicked the on/off switch once more and then pressed the button labelled "AN". Going back to the window and dragging it open, he stuck his head out and he could hear a grinding noise and a clank from the chain. He was certain he could see the anchor shifting a little. It must have been stuck in the ground for years and it was reluctant to come free, but the pull from the chain was working and Jake watched as the anchor dragged across the grass until it was lost from his view. Returning to the dashboard, he saw a green light he hadn't noticed before. Maybe it was signalling he could now try to move the house again, without the anchor holding it still.

Jake felt his heart thumping against his chest as he touched the wheel. He turned it slightly and the house slowly began to turn with it. Jake could feel his hands shaking, both from nervous excitement and the vibrations of the wheel. Almost by accident, he found the wheel could move towards him, and as he pulled it, the house started to rise. It was a slow, lazy movement, like a drift on the tide, but the house was definitely rising.

Jake looked out of the window but all he could see was the back garden. He didn't dare move the house higher in case anyone was watching at the front. He wanted to run back downstairs and look out of the front windows but didn't want to risk leaving the house floating unattended. Thinking hard, he looked around the attic room; if this was his dad's doing then there must be a way of seeing all around the house. Up in the sloping roof, he spotted what looked like a tube, hanging from one of the rafters. Scanning the control panel, he tried to remember what the tube was called but it had slipped his mind.

Reluctantly, Jake landed the house and put down the anchor again. He'd need help with this amazing discovery. It was like his dad had given him a birthday present and it made him feel as if he was bubbling over with excitement. He went downstairs and back into the garden. The house had certainly moved and was now settled in a slightly different position.

There's no way my mum knew what the house could do, Jake thought. No one would sell a house like this; maybe only his dad knew what the house could do, and how special it was. And now, so did he.

Chapter 3

Jake locked up, hid the key again because he was scared to leave it in a pocket in case he lost it, and slipped out from behind the hoardings. He tried to stroll but his feet wanted to run.

Reaching home, Jake was full of questions that he didn't feel he could ask. His grandparents inquired about the running practice and then gave him his presents, and it didn't seem like the right time to be asking about the house, particularly as he'd lied to them about where he'd been after school. So, Jake remained silent, with the secret of the house buzzing inside him, like the best present he could have received, because it seemed as if it was from his dad.

The following day, as soon as he met Shi on the corner, Jake told him all about it. He could see Shi didn't quite believe him, but when he described what had happened, it did seem rather unlikely.

After school, the two boys went to Ambridge Road, and Jake showed Shi the house.

This time, he knew what to do and started the engine (for that was what it had to be), released the anchor and slowly lifted the house a very short way up. Shi was completely silent, his face showing shock. For one rare moment, he said nothing at all. Jake settled the house back down and explained he needed to see all around the outside when he was taking the house up, and that there was what he thought might be a periscope (he'd remembered the name in the middle of the night) but he couldn't reach it or find a button to lower it. Shi stood with his mouth open and then he went to the window.

"How does it work? It's just not possible!" Shi said.

Somehow Jake had expected him to be a bit more excited, in the same way he was. Instead, Shi almost seemed to disbelieve his own eyes.

"My dad must have made it," Jake replied.

Shi snorted at that. "Was your dad an inventor? I thought he was a sailor!"

This was not playing out how Jake had imagined.

"But he must have done – who else could have done it? And that's why he wanted me to look after it, because it's special."

Shi didn't answer. He was staring out of the window at the scar the anchor had left on the grass.

"It's not possible. This house is not possible. If it was, then it would be new technology and the government would come and get it, and everyone would know," Shi said.

"It's not technology!" Jake almost shouted. "Can't you see? It's my dad's present to me and it's magic."

As soon as he said the word "magic", he realised it sounded silly and that whatever this was, it wasn't magic, at least not a fairy tale kind of magic. But it didn't seem like technology either and Jake couldn't describe what was happening.

"What are we going to do about it?" Shi asked.

Jake heard the word "we" and was very

happy that at least Shi thought they were in it together. "What *should* we do?"

"Well, we need to find out the date for demolition and rescue the house," Shi said decisively.

Jake felt suddenly cold. In all the excitement, he'd forgotten the house was set to be demolished. He couldn't let that happen. But where could you hide a house?

"We make a plan, right?" Shi said. "The first thing we do is find out when demolition day is."

Jake nodded. "And then, we work out where we're going to move the house."

They dropped anchor and slipped out of the house and back onto the street. Shi carefully noted down the builder's details. The company was called Wide Lawns, and they were planning on building luxury houses and apartments the whole way down the road. Shi got out his phone. He put on a different voice and called Wide Lawns.

"Hello, I'm calling from the council about the Ambridge Road development. Will we need to

divert traffic when you demolish the houses? … When will that be?" There was a long pause while someone went to check, and then Shi put the phone back in his pocket.

"We've got until the middle of June, then they're going to do the whole lot as quickly as they can, and they don't need the road closed."

Jake thought. "That gives us about a month to

learn how to sail the house properly and move it somewhere safe," he said.

"Next, we find a box or something to stand on," Shi announced.

Jake frowned, puzzled.

"To reach the tube thing," Shi elaborated, "the periscope. We can't move the house if we can't see where we're going. Let's hope we can pull it down a bit to see through it."

Shi was walking and talking and peering behind the hoardings to see if he could find a sturdy box. "We have a small ladder with a seat I could borrow from home."

"Won't your mum mind?" Jake asked.

"She won't notice, and I can easily carry it too; it's not heavy."

That, Jake thought, *is the easy bit.*

Chapter 4

The thing about Shi was that he was unstoppable once he'd set his mind to something. He was like that with schoolwork – if he was interested. There must have been something about the house that really grabbed him, because he set about trying to think of where to hide it straight away. He invited Jake back to his house, got out the laptop and they studied the aerial view of the town.

Jake liked looking at the maps, but Shi definitely preferred trying to find somewhere by walking around the town – "fieldwork", he called it.

That weekend, they went out walking together, looking closely at each place that had seemed empty on the aerial photos. The maps must have been out

of date as many of those places now had houses or flats built on them.

In between these expeditions, Jake went back to Toledo. He did move it a few times, not high or far, just a little lift in the garden. Shi brought the ladder, and they pulled down the periscope. This gave them vision of the area all around the house, and the periscope had the added benefit of magnifying the view.

"We don't want to bring down telephone or electricity cables when we move the house properly," Shi said.

Jake hadn't even thought about the dangers and he was surprised Shi had. He'd been so focused on finding somewhere to put the house, he'd forgotten about how they would move it, unseen, from one place to another.

Jake ran his hands over the steering wheel and moved his gaze back to the periscope. He could see the road clearly and a person coming down from the far end, walking slowly. He could see the building site across the road and thought how lucky it was that no one actually lived around here right now, so they could move the house without neighbours spotting them.

The problem of the place to hide a house was still not solved and time was passing by quite rapidly. Both boys were starting to realise they couldn't move the house too far, as the chances of it being spotted would increase with every moment they were in the air. They also realised they would have to move it at night, which would increase the likelihood of it getting caught on telephone wires or snagged on the tops of trees. There would be no headlights to light the way, and they wouldn't be able to use them, even if they had some to use.

This problem didn't stop them visiting Toledo whenever they could. They tried all the switches to see what they did and, whilst many appeared to do nothing, it was still useful to practise flying a little way off the ground and trying to land in the same place. The more they went to the house, the more marvellous it seemed. They tried to discover how it worked, if there was an engine and how the anchor chain was attached. Jake was thinking more and more like it was magic, whilst Shi was thinking that it was fantastic and futuristic technology that anyone would be glad to get their hands on.

Jake decided they needed to set up an investigation board in the attic. He didn't want them to get muddled with all the maps they were looking

at and places they'd been visiting. He started a checklist to tick off the sites they were investigating, which was rapidly being crossed off.

He also began to read his father's little notebook in detail, which was a manual of sorts for sailing the house. It was clear his father hadn't done much more than them in terms of moving the house, though there was one entry which described a brief trip above the neighbours' houses. Jake had hoped for more clues in the notebook about how the house could move and what they'd need to do to sail it properly, but it seemed as if they were going to have to solve this themselves.

Chapter 5

It was a slightly cloudy Sunday afternoon, with the sky threatening rain later. Jake and Shi had spent the entire afternoon in the house, armed with some more maps they'd got from the library. They'd spent the afternoon going through the maps in detail, studying each likely place and writing down addresses to visit during the week. They were adding to the investigation wall and had started to think of trying places further away, even though that would be far riskier.

They'd taken oat bars stuffed with dried fruit that Shi's mother had made; at that moment, it really did feel as if they'd found not just an extraordinary house but a secret den.

They were so busy making plans that they weren't as careful coming out from behind the hoardings as they might have been.

And right outside the lilac boards were Callum Grant and Harrison Smith.

"Whatcha doing there?" Callum inquired, with a slight sneer on his face. Harrison said nothing, as usual.

"Looking for a place for a den, but that's no good as it's going to be pulled down soon." Shi was really good at making up stuff to get himself out of difficult situations.

"But you've been in there for ages," Callum commented, his eyes never leaving Shi's face. It was all quite casual, but Jake knew nothing was really ever casual where Callum was concerned. Callum rarely got into trouble at school, but he often did little, unpleasant things, like kicking people, pulling people's hair, treading on others' work; never enough to get caught but enough to make Jake not trust him at all.

"We had some food. There's an overgrown garden." Shi held up the bag the oat bars had been in, with the crumbs still clearly visible. "What are you doing?"

Callum liked talking about himself. "Harrison's dad will pay us for scrap metal, but don't go getting any ideas though, this is our patch, and we don't want you collecting stuff too."

Jake looked at the little cart the other boys had;

it was like an old go-kart on a rope. It had bits and pieces of metal in it.

"I think I saw bedsprings a few doors down," Jake told them.

"Nah. Bedsprings are no good – we need chunkier stuff but smaller – we couldn't carry a bed frame back to Harrison's place." Callum paused. "Seen any metal in that house?" he asked, pointing to the hoardings outside number 63.

Jake thought of the huge anchor in the garden and the amount of metal that it would have in it. It would be too big to lift, but it wouldn't be hard to find.

Shi just shook his head and said, "We've not been in the house. It's all locked up."

The last part wasn't a lie, Jake thought. "Yeah, and there's nothing in the garden except grass and weeds," he told them.

Callum clearly guessed there was more to it than that, but walked on with Harrison, pulling the cart behind them. Once they were around the corner,

Jake allowed himself to breathe again.

"You need to take the key with you this time; we can't let them get in the house," Shi said.

Jake fetched the key and tucked it into his phone case. Then they both went into the garden to find a hiding place for the anchor. Even though they hid it behind some large shrubs, neither Shi nor Jake were convinced it was disguised enough to be really safe.

Walking home, Jake and Shi discussed what to do next. The demolition date was drawing closer all the time and it was suddenly really urgent that they find somewhere to put the house. Jake felt as if his whole relationship with his father was in jeopardy, as he couldn't even manage to do one thing his father had asked him to do. He was also worried that Callum and Harrison would find out about the house, or at the very least, damage it.

"Do you think there's a way to stop Wide Lawns from demolishing the houses so soon?" Jake thought out loud.

"Why would they stop? There's no reason; it's not as if there are people living in the houses or anything left to work out. They must be all ready to go," Shi replied.

Jake paused, and thought about all the ways demolition might be stopped or delayed.

"What if there were bats?" he said.

Shi looked at him. "Bats? Why would bats matter?"

"Bats are protected, and you can't demolish buildings or build new ones if there are bats on the site. We couldn't say it was Toledo specifically, but we could say we'd seen bats flying in and out of the houses in the road. If we can't find a place to move the house, that might delay things."

"But it would be much better to find a place before calling the bat squad," Shi said, with a grin.

Jake nodded. "And before Callum and Harrison come back."

Chapter 6

Another week went by, and the demolition was only six days away. Jake and Shi went to the house because they couldn't think of anything else to do; they'd exhausted all the places they'd thought of to hide Toledo and were now thinking about the bat idea simply because there was no other alternative.

Jake switched the engine on and gave the house a little try just before they were leaving. He loved the feel of vibrations beneath his feet and the way Toledo rose as he held the wheel. Reluctantly, he put the house back on the ground and lowered the anchor.

He glanced at the investigation wall of maps, as he was about to leave the attic. *Wait a minute,* he thought. Walking over to the maps, Jake saw what should have been perfectly obvious much, much sooner.

"Shi, I've found it!" he shouted down the stairs to Shi, who was already almost out of the front door.

Shi came running back up the stairs, panting. "Found what?"

"The perfect place, at least for a while. A place to hide the house … The park." Jake paused and pointed to the map. "The island in the park has lots

of trees and no one goes there. At the moment, the house would be hidden by the trees and that would give us time to find somewhere more permanent."

Shi looked at the map. "Why didn't we see that before?" he wondered. "It IS perfect. Not too far and look, from this photo, it even has a space in the middle to land the house. Jake, you're a genius!"

They left the house, talking through the plan as they went.

"I'm sure there's a little dinghy in the shed at home," Jake began. "We'd have to take it with us to get back off the island, once we've put the house there."

"I don't think we should wait any longer," Shi replied. "We should move the house now; what about tonight?"

Jake stopped walking and looked at Shi. He couldn't quite believe how fast things were moving and that he was going to sail the house to a new location that night. All of a sudden, problems crowded into his head. How would he navigate in the dark? There would be wires and trees and all sorts that might snag on the house if he didn't go high enough. What if there wasn't enough space to land in the park, after all, or if the house wasn't properly hidden when the sun came up?

Shi seemed to know how he was feeling. "Come and stay at my house," he offered. "Then we can go out together. My parents will never notice, and it'll be nicer than getting there on our own."

Jake nodded gratefully.

"Before we go home, I need to walk the route from the house to the park and check for tall trees or poles," Jake said, with sudden decisiveness.

"Aren't we going the shortest route, straight across to the park?" Shi queried.

"I'm not sure we can risk it, we might get lost, and it's easier to follow the roads in the dark. I'll use the map on my phone and the streetlights."

Shi nodded in agreement and the boys turned around and headed towards the park.

The route from the house to the park wasn't far but Jake could only imagine how long it would be in the dark, sailing above it all. He thought it might seem like it would last forever, particularly as he'd never sailed the house properly; little movements around the garden weren't the same thing.

The building site on the other side of the road was busy; dozens of homes were taking shape in the space where the old houses had stood. Some of them were so close together Jake thought that people in one house would be able to reach someone in the next house by leaning out from their windows. It didn't look as if any of them would have gardens, only small courtyards front and back. Jake knew that Toledo would be a building site like this if he didn't hide it tonight.

Jake got out his phone and began making notes about the trees and telephone poles. There were some very large horse-chestnut trees and a crane quite near to the road. He wondered how high he needed to take the house to avoid the trees and the buildings and then he worried that the house might not be able to go high enough. They reached the park, and Jake felt his panic rising. The park entrance said the gates closed at dusk.

Shi must have read his mind because he pointed to the fence a bit further down from the entrance and said, "It's broken there, so it'll be easy to get in and out."

The park was large and had paths that led in several directions: one towards a café, one to the lake and another to a playground. Jake noticed a few lampposts dotted along the paths and wondered if they would be on at night when the park was closed. They walked on until they reached the lake. It looked both larger and smaller than Jake had pictured it in his head.

He wondered how they could possibly row all that way back, and he also couldn't imagine the house being hidden on the island. It was true the bushes and trees were quite thick, but what if it was too thick to land or nothing was tall enough to hide the house completely? The lake was surrounded by a fence as well, but there were gaps in it that

looked large enough for them to squeeze through.

"There's nothing we can do but try it. Better that than Toledo gets knocked down. Then we have a bit of time to find a proper place to put the house. It's the only option." Shi spoke quite definitely and that helped. Jake felt the whole thing was being shared and that did make it easier than just being by himself.

They walked back, and Jake promised to come over later. Shi said his mother would insist he came for a meal and Jake said he would text once he'd cleared it with his grandparents. Jake let himself into his house; all he had to do now was find the dinghy and sneak it out without his grandparents noticing.

Chapter 7

Jake's grandmother appeared at the end of the hall and smiled when she saw him. "Grandpa's cooking," she said.

This meant the kitchen was probably covered in flour or some other mess; Grandpa's food tasted great, but he made the most mess anyone could.

"Shi has invited me over this evening to spend the night. Is that OK?" Jake asked. He knew it would be all right because it wasn't a school night.

"Wish I could come too," Grandma said. "When your grandfather starts comparing his pie-making to the battle of Waterloo, I know it's time to leave the kitchen."

Jake liked Grandpa's pies, but now was not the time to change his mind about going out that night.

Jake threw some things into an overnight bag, just pyjamas, wash things and clean underwear for the next day. He went over to Shi's for the night fairly regularly (and occasionally Shi came over to his house), so he was used to an overnight stay and knew what to pack. This time, however, Jake began to wonder if he'd need anything he didn't usually take. He decided that food might be important and slipped in some flapjacks his grandfather had made a few days before. He hoped that they'd stay in one piece – trying to eat a bag of crumbs might not be that easy while sailing a house.

Then he went out to the shed. It was quite large and slightly rickety, set at the end of the garden next to the wall. The wall was Jake's favourite place to read; it had a set of stone steps going up to the top and a view across to the ruins of Hapsworth Hall. There wasn't much left of the hall – it had been destroyed by fire and abandoned many years before – but Jake liked the view, and it was a peaceful place to sit with a book.

Grandpa had told him Hapsworth Hall had once been at the centre of vast amounts of land, but now it was all built on apart from the area immediately around the hall itself. The ruin was surrounded by a high wall with notices warning people to keep out.

The shed was full of clutter. There were gardening tools on one wall and shelves of oddments on the other: broken toasters, an old go-kart and other things Grandma had intended to fix but not got round to yet. There was also the dinghy, partly deflated. Jake pulled it down, hoping that there were no holes in it. It looked OK but he wanted to be really sure. He took it round to the side of the house and sprayed water from the garden hose into it. There didn't seem to be any leaks, and Jake breathed a sigh of relief.

He then moved the dinghy round to the front of the house and left it upside down in a corner to dry. He was just about to go back inside when he realised that he'd forgotten some essential pieces of equipment and returned to the shed.

First, he took out the oars and then hunted for the pump to blow the dinghy up properly. He couldn't find it at first, but then he spotted it

on a different shelf. He took it with the oars and left them with the dinghy, just out of sight of the front door.

A short while later, Jake came back out with his overnight bag, and after adding the oars and pump to a different bag, he set off with both bags and the dinghy to go to Shi's house.

Chapter 8

As he walked to Shi's house, Jake was grateful for the warm dry weather and the fact that he didn't need to wrap up tonight to go out. Carrying the dinghy and oars was hard work and he kept having to stop and readjust his hold on them. He was so busy thinking about how they'd manage moving the house, he was completely unaware that Callum had spotted him and was wondering what Jake could possibly be doing with a dinghy.

Shi's house was large and always seemed loud and full of conversation, switching from English to Hebrew and back again. Jake loved going over there; he loved the ordinariness of the arguing and the banter. His grandparents never argued and rarely raised their voices. He loved everyone discussing everything, from how their day had been to the weather to politics, generally all at the same time!

Today was no exception. Shi's brothers were shouting at each other over a computer game they were playing. They paused briefly to say hi to Jake and then carried on. Shi's mother was talking in Hebrew on the phone and making dinner in a noisy and chaotic kitchen. Jake couldn't see or hear Shi's father, but he must have been in the house somewhere.

Shi led Jake upstairs to put his bag down in his bedroom.

"I can't believe we're really going to do this!" Shi half whispered at Jake.

"There are so many things that might go wrong," Jake started, before they were interrupted by Shi's mother calling them down for supper.

Jake felt so nervous that he could hardly eat. The food was so good though that he found himself eating, even though the tension made him feel a bit sick. He kept catching Shi's eye and thinking about what they'd be doing in only a few hours' time. It was almost a relief to go up to bed.

He snuggled under the covers and watched as Shi set an alarm on his phone. "Won't it wake everyone, going off in the night like that?" Jake asked.

"Everyone stays up late; they'll be downstairs and no one will hear it," Shi replied.

"How will we get out if they're still up?"

"They won't hear us, just as they won't hear the alarm. We'll make a roll of clothes to look like we're in bed; Mum puts her head round the door, but she never comes in the room. Then we'll slip out of the back door. Stop worrying, everything's under control." Shi was sure and calm and that helped.

It was a good thing about the alarm, as they both fell fast asleep. As the alarm went off, Jake struggled to work out where he was. With a lurch he remembered and climbed out of bed, putting his jeans on and a thin fleece. Shi was doing the same and arranging some other clothes into a convincing shape under the covers. He did the same for Jake's bed and then they both crept out of the bedroom and down the stairs.

Shi was right about no one being able to hear them. The TV was on and there was lots of talking and arguing coming from the front room. The boys went into the kitchen and unlocked the back door. Shi then locked it from the outside and pocketed the key. Jake felt for the key to Toledo, which was now around his neck on a chain.

"Grab the dinghy and the oars," Jake whispered.

They pulled the boat out from behind the bins, where Jake had hidden it, and set off.

Walking the streets at twilight was rather different to the daytime walking they were used to. Everything seemed quiet and the streetlights had just come on. Many houses had light spilling from the front rooms and the boys felt as if they were on the outside of people's lives. It wasn't particularly cold, but Jake shivered with nerves and excitement.

Jake let himself and Shi into Toledo. It was very dark inside and they needed the torches that they'd brought. Shi held one up while Jake took a glance at his dad's manual, hoping he might find more clues there to help him sail. Then he lifted the anchor and started the engine. He brought the periscope towards him and almost to himself said, "Here goes."

The house began to rise. Jake knew they'd need to go higher than the trees in the neighbour's back garden as well as the houses. He could feel the house vibrating slightly through his feet, but the engine was remarkably quiet. They rose until Jake was more than certain they were well above all the highest points on the way. Then, slowly,

he slid the joystick forwards and with a little initial jerk, the house began to move forwards; Jake gripped the wheel and slowly started to steer the house along the road. He'd thought being up so high would be like flying, but with the gentle rocking motion it was much more like being on a boat.

Shi was pressed against the window and keeping a watch for obstacles, as well as calling out landmarks as he saw them. Jake used the periscope to try and keep the house steady above the road. He wasn't sure how fast they were moving or how difficult it would be to turn when they came to that part of the journey. His hands were shaking, and he could hear his heart thumping loudly. He found he was repeating the same thing over and over under his breath. "Look, Dad, I'm taking care of Toledo."

Shi called a warning: "I can see the junction of Prestwich Road, coming up shortly."

This was the first proper turn whilst moving. Gently Jake began to turn the wheel, but it was more responsive than he'd thought, and he'd be turning too soon if he wanted to stay along the line of the road. There was nothing he could do about it now and he cut the corner of the road, skimming the tops of the taller houses there. *One of the homeowners is going to wonder where their aerial has disappeared to*, thought Jake, as the house knocked it off the roof.

Jake decided he needed to go a little higher. Prestwich Road was full of bigger houses and taller trees, and it made him feel very nervous. Going higher whilst moving forwards resulted in more small jerky movements but he found he got the hang of it by stroking the controls gently, rather than pushing or pulling. Jake might have been imagining it, but it felt as if the house was happy, sailing free after all these years, almost skipping along the route.

The next couple of turns were much smoother and Jake almost allowed himself to feel a bit more relaxed. But he knew that the hardest part was yet to come – landing the house on an unlit island. As they flew over the park fence, Shi tried to shine his torch out of the window so they could see, but that didn't work particularly well. He opened the heavy sash window and shone the torch out of the gap, but the darkness seemed to swallow the light up, and Jake found he was guessing the direction of the lake.

There was a moment when Jake wondered what they'd do if they couldn't find the lake and then, suddenly, he saw three lines of lights fanning out and realised they must be the paths in the park. The house was moving in the direction of the children's playground so he corrected its course and then began to slow down. Meanwhile, Shi had grabbed the other torch they'd brought, the much bigger one they'd need for landing the house.

The trees on the island looked both thicker and darker from above. "Let's hope there really is room for the house," Jake said, slightly tensely.

Shi had his head right out of the window and was shining the large torch straight down. Suddenly, he saw the clearing. He started shouting and pointing the torch to a gap in the trees.

The clearing was long and looked narrow.

Jake tried to think about which way he should set the house down.

"Turn and set down sideways," Shi shouted.

Jake grabbed the periscope and manoeuvred the house until he was fairly certain it was over the gap.

"Get your head in," Jake yelled. Shi pulled his head in quickly and shut the window.

The house descended little by little. The branches scraped against the walls and the windows and, for a moment, Jake thought the house had got jammed on a branch halfway down. He was wrong; they touched down with only a slight bump. The house wasn't quite level, but Jake was able to lower the anchor and then turn off the power.

Jake and Shi looked at each other in the gloom. Without the torches, they'd have been able to see very little as the surrounding trees cut off most of the light from outside.

Shi was grinning and he slapped Jake happily on the back. "You did it! You sailed Toledo and saved it!"

They went downstairs and carefully opened the front door. The trees were pressed in around the house and for a moment they both thought they might not be able to get out. But then Jake shone his torch and revealed a gap they'd be able to squeeze through. Jake locked the house and, somehow, with the dinghy between them, they dragged themselves through the trees and out to the edge of the island.

In the dark, the lake looked huge and murky as if it had no bottom to it. In the daytime, it was quite pretty, but it changed at night.

"Is now a good time to say I've never rowed an inflatable dinghy before?" Jake said.

"Me neither," Shi admitted. "But you've just sailed a house, so how difficult can this be?"

They got wet feet straight away and at first couldn't move the dinghy away from the shore. It had seemed so simple when they'd talked about it. They did quite a bit of rowing round in circles until they began to get the hang of the rhythm, but it seemed like hours before they reached the other shore.

They arrived at the fence surrounding the lake and slipped through the gap, passing the dinghy over the top. Jake didn't even want to think about rowing across that lake again, though he knew at some point he'd have to. His arms ached and his hands felt as if they were on fire. At that point, he wasn't even sure he had the energy to walk back to Shi's house. The outer park fence was slightly harder to navigate as it was taller, but the dinghy was light enough to half throw over the top again. As they walked back, talking about what they'd just done, Jake felt his sense of achievement returning and the enthusiasm was strangely catching. They almost forgot how tired they were, as they talked about what had just happened and suggested ideas for what they were going to do next.

Shi's house was silent and dark. They crept in as quietly as they could and up to the bedroom. They peeled off still slightly damp clothes and crawled under the covers. Jake noticed that it was almost one o'clock in the morning, and then he slept.

Chapter 9

Jake and Shi slept late the following morning. They both felt weary even after sleep and both were stiff and aching from the rowing. After a late breakfast, Shi told his parents he'd walk Jake home. But first, they were going to see what Ambridge Road looked like without the house, and if there was anything left behind. Then they were going to walk to the park and check if the house was really hidden.

As they reached the row of houses due for demolition, they could see something was going on. There were lots of people standing around and a police car parked nearby. Callum broke free from the crowd and rushed towards them, yelling, "There they are. They must know something!"

A man in a high-vis jacket and hard hat approached them. "Callum here told us you might know something about number 63," he said.

"Number 63? I used to live there, when I was very little," Jake answered honestly.

"But it isn't there now," the man told him.

"Sorry? What do you mean?" Jake replied, with an innocent expression. He found to his surprise that where the house was concerned, he could lie quite easily.

The man gestured for them to follow him, and they walked past the crowd and to the now rather larger gap in the hoardings. The man pointed at the space where Toledo had been.

"It's gone," he said unnecessarily.

Shi, who was particularly good at putting on an innocent expression, responded with, "Has it been knocked down already?"

The man paused and took a deep breath. "If

it had been knocked down, there would be rubble. Can you see rubble? The house has been stolen! I want to know how this happened."

Shi laughed, which only seemed to make the man even more cross.

"How can you steal a house?" Jake asked.

"That's what I want to know!" the man continued.

Shi tilted his head, and Jake knew what was coming next. Shi had a real gift for irritating adults by stating the obvious.

"So, you think the house that you were going to knock down anyway has been stolen? And so instead of having to clear rubble, you've nothing to clear away, and you're upset about that? You also think that we stole the house? Yes, of course, we picked it up and moved it with a big digger without anyone noticing."

The man went a funny red colour. Jake noticed that he was wearing a lanyard with Wide Lawns on it. It was his company that was going to knock down the houses. But Shi had a point, why was he cross about a house that was scheduled to be knocked down anyway?

"What was it you were telling me, Callum?" the man asked.

Callum stood next to them, puffed out his chest and looked important. "I've seen them near the house; they've been acting shifty. They definitely know something."

"We've been looking for somewhere to make a den," Jake said, sticking to their story, "but we knew the house was due for demolition, so there was no point."

"Look at the signs!" the man was shouting now. "They say no entry! They say danger! The house might not have been safe; it might have collapsed on you."

Everyone was looking at them by this point and the shouting had attracted the attention of the two police officers who'd been standing at the side of the road.

"Mr Whitlock, there's no need to raise your voice. Shouting at children isn't a good look," the younger of the two police officers said, getting out his notebook. "So, let me get this straight, you've called us out because the house you were about to knock down has been stolen? I have to ask why you think these boys have anything to do with it?" He gave Callum a look. The police officer sounded more than slightly annoyed at the ridiculousness of the situation.

"Before we demolish buildings, we go in and strip out the valuable stuff we can sell on. Things like copper pipes, marble fireplaces, stained glass, old kitchens and so on. I was due to get to work on that house today. When I checked yesterday, it was there, and young Callum here, he thinks these boys know what might have happened." Mr Whitlock was very insistent, and the police officer looked a bit bemused.

"So … if I wanted to steal a house, what would I need? We need to know what we're looking for," the police officer explained. It was clear both police officers thought the whole thing was nonsense. When you looked at it that way, it really was rather ridiculous to accuse two schoolboys of stealing a whole house.

Mr Whitlock had clearly not thought about how a house could be stolen. He stood there opening and closing his mouth like a fish and then turned slowly to look at the empty plot where the house had once stood.

"Well," he started to explain. "You'd need to know the house had no foundations," he finished triumphantly.

"How would you know if the house had foundations?" the police officer asked, genuinely interested.

Mr Whitlock clearly had no idea how you would know this. He made up an answer using a few bits of jargon and obviously made-up details.

"You'd need a crane and a large lorry, and you'd lift the house onto the lorry and then drive off with it." Mr Whitlock finished, and looked at Jake and Shi accusingly, as if the two boys in front of him were going to be able to get their hands on a crane and a lorry and use them to steal a house.

"I can't drive," Shi said helpfully. "I don't

think Jake can either."

Jake shook his head.

The police officer with the notepad was trying and failing to conceal a smile.

"Right. So, we need to look at CCTV from the area and see if a lorry with a house on it has driven away from here?"

Mr Whitlock nodded vigorously, and Jake thought how lucky it was that the house would have been way above all the cameras and no one would have seen it being moved.

Meanwhile, Callum was glaring at Jake as if he could sense that this whole house moving thing was unlikely, but that he was also sure Jake and Shi were somehow involved.

"I saw you with a dinghy yesterday," he said, pointing at Jake.

"I don't think a house would fit on a dinghy," Jake replied.

But Callum wasn't giving up. "Don't worry,

Mr Whitlock, I'll find out where the house is!" The police officer uttered something similar, but they didn't seem to be taking it seriously.

Callum looked at them and Jake felt a chill. It was clear that Callum would keep on trying to find the house, that he was certain he was onto something and wouldn't give up until he'd found out what they were up to.

Jake had thought the house would be safe until the leaves started to fall from the trees and only then would they have to think about moving it again, but now he wasn't so sure.

Shi must have seen his face because, as they walked away, he said, "You know Callum will never guess what really happened."

Almost as soon as the words were out of his mouth, Callum appeared right next to them; his ears must have been sharper than Shi had given him credit for.

"Oh? So, what really happened?" Callum asked. He had a nasty sneer on his face, as if he'd caught them out, which of course he had.

"There was a tornado last night and the house blew away just like in the Wizard of Oz. It's now sitting in the school playground!" retorted Shi, as quick as a flash. Jake could never work out how Shi came up with the stories he told, as quickly as he did.

Callum appeared to find this explanation entirely plausible, so he ran off in the direction of school, not even stopping to think how unlikely it might be. Neither Jake nor Shi said a word until Callum was out of sight and they were in the park, sitting on a bench looking across the lake.

Chapter 10

Jake had to admit that right now the house was very well hidden. The trees and bushes were very thick, and the house didn't show at all.

"You do know that Callum isn't going to stop bothering us? He seems to know we're involved, even if he can't work out how," Jake began.

"He'll never find Toledo. He's got no imagination. He'll never work out that the house just sailed away," Shi replied confidently.

"I know that, but he's really persistent, like a terrier. He'll follow us around and keep on at us and we still need to find a proper place to hide the house before the leaves fall off the trees. We're not much further forward than we were before, we just have a little more time to find a place." Jake was worried, even though they'd snatched the house away just in time.

They walked back towards Jake's home. They needed to get on with their investigation and look again at where they might hide Toledo.

Jake turned out to be right about Callum. With Harrison as his shadow, Callum started methodically walking the streets looking for the house. He might not have known what really happened, but even he could see that a house couldn't vanish entirely overnight; it must be somewhere. He was also certain that the dinghy had something to do with it, though he had no idea what the connection might be. Every breaktime at school, he and Harrison would sidle over to Jake and Shi and try to listen to their conversation. Then he started to follow them home from school. The only chance they got to talk in peace was on the way to school or when they were in their own homes.

Every once in a while, Mr Poppard encouraged the class to ask him questions. Jake decided that this would be a good opportunity to see if he could solve the problem of the house, but he knew he couldn't ask directly about it.

"Mr Poppard, how can you hide an elephant?" he asked.

Some of the class laughed, but Mr Poppard

looked thoughtful. "Well, Jake, excellent question ... You hide an elephant among other elephants," Mr Poppard said. Which of course made perfect sense. Something tickled around the edge of Jake's mind, an idea he couldn't quite catch hold of.

After school, walking home, Jake and Shi decided to look at the maps again. As far as Jake could see, it was the fact that houses don't just spring up out of nowhere that was the problem. They were so deep in conversation, they both missed the fact that Callum was right behind them, with Harrison as always.

"Ha! I knew it!" Callum shouted, in triumph.

Jake thought quickly about what Callum might have heard. He was certain they'd not mentioned where the house was, but what else might he have overheard?

"What do you know, Callum?" Shi asked, sighing slightly.

"You stole the house!" Callum crowed.

"Do you know how silly that sounds? How could

we steal a house?" Shi retorted.

"I don't know how you stole it, but I know that you did," Callum said. "I know it has something to do with that dinghy you had too, and I *will* find out!"

Chapter 11

Jake picked at his food that night; he looked so gloomy, his grandparents noticed.

"Mr Poppard phoned us this week," his grandfather began. "He's worried about you. He says you're not quite yourself. He wondered if there's something worrying you?"

Jake froze, briefly wondering if he should say something. He shook his head. "I'm just tired and looking forward to the holidays." He could see his grandparents didn't believe that for a moment.

As soon as he was able, Jake met Shi. They both went to the park and Jake told him how close he'd been to telling his grandparents everything.

Shi nodded and said he felt that way sometimes.

"It feels like such a responsibility to look after the house like my dad asked; I just don't want to let him down," Jake said.

Shi reassured him that he was doing a great job and wasn't letting anyone down.

They began to discuss what they should do next. Jake was going over and over what Mr Poppard had said. He was certain it was the key to solving their problem.

"I think we've been looking at this the wrong way. We've been looking for somewhere empty to put the house but, as Mr Poppard said, the best place to hide it is among other houses." Jake had an idea forming in his mind, but he couldn't quite say what the idea was yet.

"But people would notice if a house suddenly appeared," Shi argued. "They'd see a house that wasn't there the day before and think it was impossible that it could appear overnight."

Jake stood absolutely still as the idea suddenly

made sense. "What if there was a perfect place near other houses that had been there all along, but we never thought of it?"

Jake grabbed Shi and said they needed to get back to the maps, and also look up a few things, but he was sure he'd found the place.

They half ran back to Jake's house, with Shi still not knowing what solution Jake had found. Jake ran to his computer and started searching for a local map. Then he took Shi to the window that overlooked the back garden.

"It's literally been staring me in the face the whole time. Hapsworth Hall. No one can go there, and we can hide Toledo *within* the ruined walls, and no one can see it," Jake told Shi.

A broad grin spread across Shi's face. "Brilliant! A house hidden by another house! Does anyone own the land?" he asked.

"Let's find out," Jake said. "I don't want to find the perfect place and then have more demolition plans to deal with."

Both of them sat and read some information about Hapsworth Hall on the computer. It had been built more than 300 years ago but left abandoned and in ruins for over 50 years. It didn't seem to be owned by anyone but couldn't be knocked down because it was a historical building.

"It was owned by Lord Hapsworth, who was in shipping," Shi read. "The devastating fire in 1970 meant that the house was abandoned. The 15th Lord Hapsworth had no children, so most of the land was sold off … hey, that must mean your grandparents' house is built on the land!"

"There's a huge wall all around the ruins and I think we're the only ones with stairs over the wall," Jake told him. "Grandpa always thought it was because it was a shortcut into town for people from the hall."

Jake and Shi also studied the aerial view very carefully. It was almost impossible to tell if there was room inside Hapsworth Hall for the house to fit, or if it was full of rubble. Jake was also a bit nervous that it might fall down if they tried to land in it.

"We'll have to go and see it," Shi said. "We can use the steps and go over the wall and see if it's as good as it looks. It's funny that you see it every day but didn't think of it first."

The next day after school, Shi came over to Jake's house again, this time with the stepladder, as Jake had realised that they wouldn't be able to climb back over the wall without it. They climbed the steps next to the shed and then carefully let themselves down the other side. Jake was worried that someone in one of the other houses might see them walking across to the ruin, but Shi reckoned there were enough trees and shrubs from the long-abandoned gardens to hide them.

At the furthest edges, by the high outer wall, it was clear someone had cut the grass as far as the old low wall where the formal gardens started. After that, there were old paths, but it was all very overgrown, and Jake was relieved to see that no one had trampled the grass recently.

Hapsworth Hall must have once been very

grand indeed: a perfect square with at least three storeys and rows of windows. It was possible to see where the fire had scorched the edge of the windows, and there was now a tree growing out of the front door.

Jake and Shi crept up to the windows and peered inside. They were expecting to see all the rubble from the roof and inner walls; instead, it was empty apart from a few grassy patches and some small trees. The walls were being held up by huge wooden struts and they could see it was no longer a perfect square. Part of the far wall had tumbled down, and chunks of brickwork lay across the gap.

"It's just right," Jake found himself whispering. "It will fit the house with plenty of room to spare."

Even the thought of rowing back across the lake didn't take away Jake's happiness at finding somewhere to keep the house safe.

They walked back to Jake's house, noticing that the wall was too high for them to be seen by anyone other than people in Jake's house. It was

only that part of the wall that had stairs across it and was lower than the rest. Jake thought about the incredible stroke of luck that had made it all possible; that the steps were in his garden and no one else's.

They used the stepladder to climb back into the garden and then realised they couldn't lift the ladder back up again. Shi thought his parents probably wouldn't notice it was missing, which was just as well, really.

Chapter 12

Jake and Shi started to make plans to move the house again. It had to be a weekend, or they wouldn't be able to have a sleepover at Jake's house. Jake wanted to get it done sooner rather than later; all he wanted was for the house to be safely hidden where no one would find it.

The day of the sleepover and moving the house was wet and grey. Shi said that they'd get wet anyway rowing across the lake, so rain didn't really matter. Jake, who'd been dreading the rowing, felt he was wishing the day away, longing to get it all done.

It wasn't quite as easy at Jake's house to get out in the night. His grandparents set an alarm downstairs, and the back door was locked and bolted. They'd have to wait for Jake's grandparents to go to sleep, as they couldn't let them set the alarm after the boys had left, and Jake needed the key from the back door too. But Shi and Jake agreed it didn't make sense to stay at Shi's house and then have to return there once they'd left Toledo inside Hapsworth Hall.

That night, Jake's grandparents seemed to take forever to go to bed. Jake found he couldn't sleep, though Shi was softly snoring. He got up and slipped behind the curtains to look out at Hapsworth Hall. It wasn't quite dark, and the hall looked as if it was disappearing into the gloom. Toledo would be completely invisible inside the ruins and, not for the first time, Jake wished he'd thought of it sooner.

As soon as his grandparents had been in bed for half an hour, Jake woke up Shi. They dressed quickly and tiptoed down the stairs to the alarm pad. Jake was hoping that the bleep of the alarm being unset wouldn't be too loud. It echoed in the silence but there was no stirring from upstairs. The door being unbolted sounded even louder, but again his grandparents appeared to sleep through it.

The streets were empty and the pavement was damp. Jake and Shi carried the dinghy between them, hoping they wouldn't meet anyone as it would be hard to explain why they were carrying a dinghy in the middle of the night. They thought they were unseen, but that wasn't actually the case. That particular night, Callum couldn't sleep. He was looking out of the window and saw Jake and Shi walking past. He quickly pulled his shoes on and grabbed a coat and started to follow them, correctly guessing they were heading for the park.

Jake was shivering with nerves. His hands tingled with the memory of the blisters from last time they'd rowed, and Shi had lost a bit of his usual bravado. Jake put the dinghy in the water and held onto the oars as they both got in. Just like last time, they were wet straight away. Unlike last time, they had no lights to guide them in the right direction; all the park lights were behind them. But somehow, they steered towards the island, even though it seemed to take forever before they could see land in the darkness.

They dragged themselves and the dinghy up on the shore and began looking for a way through to the house. It was so completely surrounded by plants and brambles; they had another prickly journey to reach the front door. Once inside, Jake quickly got to work, lifting the house clear of the trees and then sailing it across the park towards his own home. Shi was almost silent on that journey, but his face was alive and animated with the excitement of sailing again. The house drifted across the sky, heading towards the dark patch that was the ruins of Hapsworth Hall.

If they'd looked down into the park, they would have seen Callum, standing with his mouth open, watching the house as it sailed over the park. Callum did try to follow it, but it went too quickly, and he lost sight of it before he'd climbed through the gap in the fence and left the park. He also took photos on his phone, but they showed nothing at all in the dark. No one ever believed him when he told them what he'd seen; even Harrison told him to stop talking nonsense.

Epilogue

It was the end of the summer holidays and Jake was sitting on the steps at the end of his garden, reading. His grandfather came and joined him, and they sat silently for a while.

"That was a really clever place to put it, Jake," Grandpa said, as he looked across to Hapsworth Hall.

Jake felt his face flush bright red, and he wondered what he should say in reply, but his grandfather carried on.

"I saw you that night. I couldn't sleep, so I was looking out of the window and I saw strange lights in the sky. They came down into Hapsworth Hall and, a little while later, you and Shi climbed over

the wall. The next day, I went to see for myself. It was rather a shock to see your old house sitting inside the ruins of Hapsworth Hall. No wonder your father loved Toledo. It was an excellent place to hide it."

Grandpa paused and looked at Jake. "Why don't you tell me all about it?"

So, Jake did.

Sometimes, on particularly dark nights, if you happen to glance up, you might spot the house as it sails over the rooftops, and circles back towards the ruins of Hapsworth Hall.

Book talk questions

What do you think the house represents for Jake and his family?

How does Jake's relationship with his grandparents influence the story?

Would you have done anything differently to Jake and Shi?

How do you think Jake's friends and family help him overcome obstacles?

What advice would you give to readers who have lost or been separated from a loved one?

What role does the letter from Jake's dad play in motivating him to take action?

If you had a magical house like Jake's, where would you sail to and why?

How does the house's magic change Jake's life?

What makes the adventure in *The House That Sailed Away* so unique?

What do you think will happen next for Jake and Shi?

Ask the author

What was your favourite part of the book to write?

I loved the idea of sailing a house in the dark. It was really fun to think of all the obstacles they might encounter on the way. You wouldn't believe how much is up high above your head until you start planning a journey like that!

Jacqueline Harris

Do you have a favourite illustration from the book?

The first picture of Jake and Shi. I couldn't believe Alan Brown had recreated them exactly how I had imagined them.

What do you most want readers to take away from reading this book?

To think that the impossible might be just around the corner and that you can manage to deal with it.

How did you come up with the idea of a house that sails away?

I dreamt it - I literally had a dream about the whole story minus the very end. I just had to write it down.

How did you get into writing?

I have always written stories, since I was very young and could first write. It is just something I seem to need to do. I still have piles of files with handwritten stories I wrote as a child and teenager.

Who's your favourite character in the book?

I love Jake but possibly care more about Shi because he is based on a real child I once taught. That child was very similar to Shi, in that he was impossibly cheeky and yet so charming and kind at the same time. He even had the same floppy hair.

What was your favourite book as a child?

I loved and still love *Anne of Green Gables*. I also adored *The Dark is Rising* by Susan Cooper and anything by Diana Wynne Jones.

What would you do with a house you could sail?

If my current home turned out to be able to sail it might make it very tricky to hide, but it would be such fun. My children could have birthday parties in the sky, and no one would ever believe it when their child came home and told them the party involved sailing the house to the local park!

Published by Collins
An imprint of HarperCollins*Publishers*

The News Building
1 London Bridge Street
London SE1 9GF
UK

Macken House
39/40 Mayor Street Upper
Dublin 1
D01 C9W8
Ireland

© HarperCollins*Publishers* Limited 2025

10 9 8 7 6 5 4 3 2 1

ISBN 978-0-00-874484-7

All rights reserved. No part of this publication may be reproduced, stored in a retrieval system, or transmitted in any form by any means, electronic, mechanical, photocopying, recording or otherwise, without the prior written permission of the Publisher or a licence permitting restricted copying in the United Kingdom issued by the Copyright Licensing Agency Ltd, 5th Floor, Shackleton House, 4 Battle Bridge Lane, London SE1 2HX.

Without limiting the author's and publisher's exclusive rights, any unauthorised use of this publication to train generative artificial intelligence (AI) technologies is expressly prohibited. HarperCollins also exercise their rights under Article 4(3) of the Digital Single Market Directive 2019/790 and expressly reserve this publication from the text and data mining exception.

British Library Cataloguing-in-Publication Data
A catalogue record for this publication is available from the British Library.

Author: Jacqueline Harris
Illustrator: Alan Brown (Advocate Art)
Publisher: Laura White
Commissioning editor: Holly Woolnough
Development editor: Zoë Clarke
Product manager: Holly Woolnough
Content editor: Selin Akca
Copyeditor: Sally Byford
Proofreader: Catherine Dakin
Reviewer: Lisa Davis
Cover designer: Sarah Finan
Internal design: 2Hoots Publishing Services Ltd
Typesetter: Jouve India Ltd
Production controller: Katharine Willard

p100 © Keith Harris

Collins would like to thank the teachers and children at Grange Primary School, Southwark, for being part of the development of Big Cat Read On.

Printed in the UK.

MIX
Paper | Supporting responsible forestry
FSC™ C007454

This book contains FSC™ certified paper and other controlled sources to ensure responsible forest management.

For more information visit: www.harpercollins.co.uk/green

Made with responsibly sourced paper and vegetable ink

Scan to see how we are reducing our environmental impact.

Get the latest Collins Big Cat news at
collins.co.uk/collinsbigcat